MOOMIN

and the
Favourite Thing

BASED ON THE ORIGINAL STORIES BY

Tove Jansson

PUFFIN

It was the first warm day of spring. The winter snow had melted away and everything in Moominvalley was fresh and new.

Moomin had woken early, his heart pounding with excitement. Snufkin had been away all winter, but today was the day he had promised to return. They would sail reed boats on the river and everything would be the same as before.

"Pee-hoo, pee-hoo, pee-hoo,"
sang Moomintroll quietly
to himself as he trotted
down towards the river.

Moomintroll sat on the bridge, swinging his legs and waited. He waited that day and the next day and the next, but there was neither sight nor sound of his best friend.

When *M*oomintroll could bear it no longer, he went to visit Too-Ticky.

Too-Ticky had spent the winter in the bathing hut and was giving it a spring clean, but she stopped when she saw Moomin's troubled face.

"Hello, Moomintroll," she called. "Is Snufkin back?"

"No," replied Moomin anxiously. "I'm at my wit's end waiting for him."

Too-Ticky understood at once. She fetched a long box from a pile of belongings neatly stacked on the landing stage.

"Here," she said, "take my telescope. You can watch for Snufkin with it. I'll be off to Lonely Island for the summer and I won't be needing it there. Would you look after it for me until I get back?"

"Yes," said Moomintroll, proud to be given custody of such a special thing. "I promise." And off he ran with renewed hope.

Back at the bridge Moomintroll found Thingumy and Bob. They were shy little creatures who had arrived in Moominvalley carrying a suitcase and speaking a strange language that Moomintroll had only just learned to understand.

"Hello, Troominmoll," said Thingumy. "We're going to help you snait for Wufkin."
    "Yes," said Bob, and added curiously, "What's gat you've thot?"

"It's a telescope," said Moomintroll. "It will help bring Snufkin back more quickly."

"A letescope?" whispered Thingumy and Bob at the same time.

Moomin showed them how it worked so that things far away seemed very close indeed. Then he climbed the tall tree and settled down to wait.

Around lunchtime, when he was just thinking about eating the sandwiches Moominmamma had packed for him, Moomintroll pricked up his ears. Far away in the distance he thought he could hear Snufkin's flute.

Moomintroll's heart leapt with anticipation. He turned the telescope towards the light-hearted sound . . .

... and there was Snufkin!

He was strolling along under
his old green hat, with not
a care in the world!

With Snufkin back in Moominvalley,
Moomin was as happy as he had ever been.
The sun rose earlier, the moon rose later,
and the short spring days lengthened into
a long and dreamy summer.

At first, Moomintroll took the telescope
everywhere with him and every day it
brought them new adventures.

It showed them the furthest-away ships on the horizon and led them to the ripest red berries in the forest.

And once it *even* gave them warning of an angry Antlion stalking them before breakfast!

But, as the summer wore on, they seemed to need the telescope less and less, and he'd leave it behind in the Moominhouse more and more. Then, one morning towards the beginning of autumn, Moomintroll noticed that the telescope was gone.

He looked for it everywhere, but it was nowhere to be found.

"Why worry? It's just a *thing*," said Snufkin when Moomintroll confided in him. Snufkin didn't care much for possessions.

"That's not the point," replied Moomin. "It doesn't belong to me. I promised to look after it for Too-Ticky and now I've lost it."

"Well, I think it's been stolen," said Little My at dinner that evening, and she looked meaningfully at Thingumy and Bob.

"Think what you like," said Moomintroll, shocked, "but you can't just go around accusing people!"

Secretly, though, he did wonder and, more worried than ever, he trailed upstairs to bed without even saying goodnight.

Later, Thingumy and Bob went to find Moominmamma. "Thoo you dink the letescope really has been stolen?" asked Thingumy.

"*Steally* rolen . . .?" said Bob anxiously.

Moominmamma patted her knee and they climbed on to her lap. "Well, if someone *has* taken it," she said kindly, "I feel sure they thought they were just *borrowing* it. So if they were to give it back, everything would be all right again."

Bob looked at Thingumy,
        and Thingumy looked at Bob.

The next morning, Moomintroll was sitting on the step, thinking worried *where-can-it-be?* kinds of thoughts, when he saw Thingumy and Bob carrying a familiar long box.

Solemnly, they opened it and inside, on a nest of feathers and silk, lay the telescope.

"Fe wound it," said Thingumy sadly.

"We did," said Bob. "But we didn't steal it, deally we ridn't. We just kept it safe for you because it's our thavourite fing, you see . . ."

"Our *thery* vavourite fing," said Thingumy.

And, exhausted by this long explanation, they hung their heads and looked very sorrowful indeed.

Moomin was so happy to have the telescope back that he almost laughed out loud. But he knew that this was a serious matter so he kissed Thingumy and Bob on the nose instead and they all went inside for breakfast.

"Told you!" crowed Little My when she saw Moomintroll with the telescope and Thingumy and Bob trailing behind.

"Told me what?" demanded Moomintroll airily. "Thingumy and Bob found it and now they deserve a reward! So I think we'll share the telescope until Too-Ticky comes back. I shall take care of it most of the time . . .

and Thingumy and Bob shall take care of it on Thursdays!"

"Oh!" whispered Thingumy.

"Ho!" whispered Bob. And they put their hands over their ears in wonder.

"Mank you, Thoomintroll!" they said.

"Does mat thean we can climb the trall tee and shout 'Ship ahoy'?" asked Thingumy.

"Yes," said Moomintroll. "Although I shall have to settle you in."

"And take a lacked punch and stay up there all day?" asked Bob.

"Yes," said Moomintroll.

"Wow honderful!" sighed Thingumy.

"But Thursday is always so fery var away . . ." said Bob wistfully. "Pot a wity!"

"That's true," agreed Moomintroll. "But you never know, Thursday *may* be as close as tomorrow . . ."

... and, would you believe, it *was*!

And, would you believe, it was *also* on a Thursday that a small boat appeared on the horizon, and Thingumy shouted "Hoy aship!" and Bob squeaked in excitement and dropped their lunch. Then they scrambled down the tree and rushed to the shore, to wait for Too-Ticky and to welcome her home.